PUFFIN BOOKS

Sheltie and the Runaway

Make friends with

 Sheltie®

The little pony with the big heart

Sheltie is the lovable little Shetland pony with a big personality. He is cheeky, full of fun and has a heart of gold. His best friend and new owner is Emma, and together they have lots of exciting adventures.

Share Sheltie and Emma's adventures in

Peter Clover was born and went to school in London. He was a storyboard artist and illustrator before he began to put words to his pictures. He enjoys painting, travelling, cooking and keeping fit, and lives on the coast in Somerset.

Sheltie and the Runaway

Peter Clover

PUFFIN BOOKS

PUFFIN BOOKS

Published by the Penguin Group
Penguin Books Ltd, 80 Strand, London WC2R 0RL, England
Penguin Putnam Inc., 375 Hudson Street, New York, New York 10014, USA
Penguin Books Australia Ltd, 250 Camberwell Road, Camberwell, Victoria 3124, Australia
Penguin Books Canada Ltd, 10 Alcorn Avenue, Toronto, Ontario, Canada M4V 3B2
Penguin Books India (P) Ltd, 11 Community Centre, Panchsheel Park, New Delhi – 110 017, India
Penguin Books (NZ) Ltd, Cnr Rosedale and Airborne Roads, Albany, Auckland, New Zealand
Penguin Books (South Africa) (Pty) Ltd, 24 Sturdee Avenue, Rosebank 2196, South Africa

Penguin Books Ltd, Registered Offices: 80 Strand, London WC2R 0RL, England

www.penguin.com

Sheltie and the Runaway first published in Puffin Books 1996
Sheltie Finds a Friend first published in Puffin Books 1996
This edition published 2002
1

Created by Working Partners Ltd, London W6 0HE

The moral right of the author/illustrator has been asserted

Filmset in 14/20 Palatino

Made and printed in England by Clays Ltd, St Ives plc

British Library Cataloguing in Publication Data
A CIP catalogue record for this book is available from the British Library

ISBN 0–141–31388–9

Contents

Sheltie and the Runaway

For Lynda, Albert,
Matthew and Jennifer

Chapter One

Emma was in the paddock trying
to plait Sheltie's tail into a neat,
tidy braid. Sheltie was trying to
pinch the carrot which was sticking
out of Emma's jacket pocket. After
a lot of giggling from Emma and
loud snorting from Sheltie, the
little Shetland pony came out as
the winner.

With a toss of his head, Sheltie

3

galloped off in a mad dash around the paddock. The carrot dangled from his mouth and his eyes shone, full of fun and mischief, beneath his long fringe.

'Sheltie, come back here!' Emma shouted across the paddock. Sheltie stood there, flicking his tail as he munched the carrot.

Emma had heard that a new family had moved into Fox Hall Manor on the other side of the orchard. The Armstrongs had gone to live in the city.

Mum had said that the new people had a little girl. A little girl about the same age as Emma. The postman had seen her when the removal men were unloading the furniture van the day before.

Emma was looking forward to making a new friend. She wanted Sheltie to look his very best. That was why she had been trying to plait his tail.

But Sheltie thought it was a game and wouldn't keep still. In the end, Emma gave up and left his tail just as it was: long, straggly and almost touching the ground.

Emma put on Sheltie's saddle and bridle, then rode him up the lane towards Fox Hall Manor. They passed Mr Crock's cottage, then crossed the little stream by the bridge at the end of the lane. The road curved around behind open fields and the orchard until it almost met the woods at the back of Mr Brown's meadow.

There, a long gravel drive wound its way up to a high wall with heavy iron gates. The gates were closed.

Emma rode right up and peered through the gates into the grounds of the manor.

Fox Hall was a grand place. The gardens were beautiful, with lawns and trees and flower beds planted out like a park. The gravel drive led from the iron gates up through the gardens to the front door.

The place looked deserted. Emma couldn't see any sign of the new people. She looked very hard, peering through the gates. Sheltie looked too. He pushed his nose through the bars and sniffed at the air. Sheltie could smell another pony.

Just then, Emma heard the sound of a car racing up the gravel drive behind them. When the driver slammed on the brakes to stop, the little car skidded sideways on the loose gravel and ended up with its back wheel stuck in a shallow, muddy dip.

The car door flew open and a very red-faced man jumped out. He looked at the wheel stuck in the mud, then gave the tyre a hard kick. He was in a very bad mood.

The man glanced over at Emma. He looked very grumpy.

'I thought you were Sally, my daughter,' he said. 'I thought she was outside the gates on her pony. That's not allowed!'

'Oh!' said Emma. 'I'm not Sally. My name's Emma and this is Sheltie.'

'I know you're not Sally, you silly girl. For a moment I just thought you looked like her.' He really was a grump. 'And look what you've made me do!' he said. The man looked at his car again, and stood with his hands on his hips.

Emma didn't think the accident was her fault, but she decided it would be rude to say so.

'If you have a rope,' said Emma, 'Sheltie can pull your car out of that dip.'

The man looked Sheltie up and down.

'What, that little thing?' he said. 'He doesn't look big enough to pull a baby's pram.'

'Sheltie may be small,' said Emma, 'but he's very strong. If you fetch a rope we'll show you.'

The man had a rope in the boot of the car. Emma dismounted and tied

one end of the rope to the front of the
car. Then she tied the other end
around Sheltie's chest.

'Come on, Sheltie,' whispered
Emma. 'We'll show him!'

The man started the engine. Sheltie
pulled. Emma held on to his reins
and Sheltie pulled as hard as he could.

The car moved, just a centimetre or

so at first. And then, as Sheltie pulled harder, the back wheel came right up out of the dip.

The man quickly unlocked the gates then pulled the rope free and jumped back into the car. 'Stand clear!' he shouted. Then he drove the car through and closed the gates behind him.

Emma stood with Sheltie on the other side of the gates. The man hadn't even stopped to say thank you. He was very rude.

As the man drove off up the drive, Emma saw a girl come out the house. She stood on the front steps and looked down towards the gates. Emma gave a friendly wave and the girl waved back.

Then the car pulled up at the house and the man got out and led the girl back inside.

'That must have been Sally,' said Emma. Sheltie's ears pricked up. 'She looked nice, didn't she?'

Sheltie gave a loud blow and sniffed at the air, Sheltie was more interested in the new pony he could smell.

Chapter Two

Back at the cottage Emma told Mum all about the rude and grumpy man.

'You mustn't call him names, Emma,' said Mum. 'That must have been Mr Jones. He was probably very worried if he thought Sally was locked out of the grounds.'

'He didn't say she was *locked* out,' said Emma. 'He said she wasn't allowed to *be* out.'

'Well, they did only move in yesterday,' said Mum. 'Perhaps he was afraid that Sally might wander off and get lost.'

'You can't get lost in Little Applewood!' laughed Emma. And Mum agreed.

Later that afternoon, Emma and Sheltie were practising their jumping in the paddock. Dad had rolled an old wooden barrel out into the paddock and Emma wanted to take Sheltie over it.

The wooden barrel was only half a metre high. Sheltie flew over it like a bird. Emma was sure he could have jumped over six barrels. Well, maybe two!

Emma pretended she was a

champion show jumper just like the ones she had seen on TV. She concentrated very hard and took Sheltie over the barrel again and again.

'Well done, Sheltie.' Emma leaned forward and gave him a good pat. 'You're fantastic.'

Sheltie gave a loud snort and looked very pleased with himself.

Emma kept thinking about the new family that had moved into Fox Hall Manor. She wished that she had been able to meet Sally, and say hello properly. But Emma thought it would be very difficult to make friends if Mr Jones was around.

Emma asked Sheltie what he thought.

Sheltie shook his mane and flicked his long straggly tail. Sheltie knew there was a pony hidden away somewhere. A new pony up at the manor and, like Emma, Sheltie was looking forward to making a new friend. He went frisky just thinking about it.

Emma decided to make another visit to Fox Hall Manor. It would be at least another hour before tea was ready. There was plenty of time to ride down the lane and around the back meadow to the manor house.

They skirted the woods and soon came to the gravel drive.

Emma sat on Sheltie outside the big gates and peered through the bars into the grounds. There was no sign of Sally, or anyone else. It was a very big house for just three people to live in, thought Emma. There must be at least twenty rooms.

As Emma sat there, counting the windows, Sally came around the side of the house riding a pony. A lovely black and white pony with a long white mane. Sally saw Emma standing by the gate and immediately came trotting over.

'Hello,' she said. 'My name's Sally and this is Minnow.'

Sheltie held his head high, gave a snort and flicked his tail.

Sheltie was very interested in Minnow. He poked his nose through the gates and rubbed muzzles with the black and white pony.

'This is Sheltie and I'm Emma.'

The two girls smiled at each other.
They were both about the same age
and both had blonde hair, although
Sally's was much longer than
Emma's and was tied in a plait.

The two girls liked each other
straight away.

'Sheltie looks very cheeky,' said Sally. 'I bet you have lots of fun with him.' Sally reached through the gate and stroked Sheltie's nose. His eyes twinkled beneath his bushy fringe and he gave a friendly blow.

'Minnow looks nice too,' said Emma. 'I bet you have just as much fun when you're out riding!'

Sally shook her head.

'Minnow's a lovely pony, but I'm not allowed to ride him outside. My father says we have to stay inside the manor grounds.'

'But once you know your way around Little Applewood you'll be able to come out riding, won't you?' asked Emma. 'I'll show you all the bridle paths, so you won't get lost.'

'I don't think so,' said Sally. 'It was the same in the old house. Daddy would never let me ride outside in case Minnow ran off or I had an accident.'

'But Minnow looks such a quiet pony,' said Emma. 'I can't imagine him running off.'

'That's what I think too! But Daddy has a friend whose little girl was badly hurt in a riding accident. So he doesn't want me to ride outside. You can come and ride inside, though,' added Sally. 'At least, I think you can. I'll have to ask first. Can you come back in the morning?'

Emma said she would. It was the half-term holiday, so she could come as often as Sally liked.

Emma watched Sally ride away across the grass. She wondered what Mr Jones would say when Sally asked him. She hoped it would be all right.

On the way back home Emma passed Mr Crock's cottage. Mr Crock was sitting with Fred Berry on a little wooden bench outside in the garden. Emma gave the two men a friendly wave as she and Sheltie trotted by.

Emma remembered how unfriendly Mr Crock had been when they had first met. Things had changed since she'd got to know him better, and Emma hoped that maybe it would be the same with Mr Jones.

They arrived back at the paddock just as Mum came out of the cottage to call Emma in for tea. Emma was looking forward to telling Mum all about Sally and Minnow. And even more, she was looking forward to riding in the manor grounds tomorrow.

And so was Sheltie – Emma was certain.

Chapter Three

The next morning Emma was really excited. She had breakfast early, gulping down her cereal. Then she fed Sheltie and put on his saddle, ready to go off up to the manor to visit Sally.

Emma told Sheltie to be on his best behaviour. It was important that they made a good impression on Mr Jones. After all, he hadn't been that friendly when they first met.

Sally was waiting with Minnow at the big gates. She was very pleased to see Emma.

'Mummy says it's OK if you and Sheltie come in,' said Sally. 'We can ride all morning. Daddy wasn't too pleased, but as long as we behave and don't go outside he won't mind.'

Sally jumped down from the saddle and pulled open the gates. Emma and Sheltie quickly hurried through and Sally closed the gates after them.

The grounds of Fox Hall Manor were like one huge garden which spread all around the big house. There were lawns and trees and even a pond with a statue in the middle. The statue was of a big swan standing with its wings spread out as though it were about to fly off. Water spouted from its open beak and trickled into the pond.

Emma noticed that wire netting had been fixed across the water. Sally said her father had fitted the netting in case of an accident.

Emma thought Mr Jones was a bit funny. He seemed to be always worrying that something would happen to Sally. She wasn't allowed to ride outside or to have any fun. Emma thought it was very sad.

At the bottom of the grounds was a nice flat open meadow. Minnow had his stable down there. It was a proper wooden stable with doors and a cobblestone yard where Sally could groom Minnow until his coat shone like satin. He already looked like a show pony.

Next to Minnow, Sheltie looked hairy and untidy with his long straggly mane and tail. But Sheltie was a Shetland pony and Emma liked the way he looked.

In the meadow, two jumps were set up. They were real pony jumps made of wood and brush. But they were very low, not even as high as Sheltie's barrel.

The two girls rode their ponies round and took the two jumps one after the other. Sheltie was showing off in front of Minnow and jumping much higher than he needed to.

Emma told Sally how she made her

own jump with bricks and a plank of
wood. Sheltie could jump six bricks
high. Sally thought it sounded really
wonderful.

Then Emma told Sally all about Little Applewood. She told Sally about Horseshoe Pond and the woods behind Prickly Thicket. And when she told Sally about the rolling downs and the open countryside Emma noticed a sad look on Sally's face.

'It must be lovely to ride out all on your own across the countryside,' said Sally.

'It is,' said Emma.

'I don't think I'll ever be allowed to ride outside,' said Sally.

'Well, maybe one day,' said Emma.

She was glad her mum and dad were not like Mr Jones, never letting her go anywhere.

When it was time for Emma to go home she suddenly had an idea.

'Would your dad let you come over to our cottage for tea?' said Emma.

Sally's face lit up with a big bright smile. 'That would be wonderful,' she said. 'I'll have to wait for the right moment to ask. I would really like to come.'

Emma hoped that Mr Jones would say yes.

When Emma left, Sally stood with Minnow at the big gates and watched Emma ride away on Sheltie. Sheltie's tail was swishing from side to side and Minnow gave a little whimper. He didn't seem to want his new friend to go and neither did Sally. She decided to ask right there and then if she could go and visit Emma for tea.

*

Later that afternoon, Mrs Jones telephoned from Fox Hall Manor and spoke to Emma's mum. Sally was allowed to come over for tea the following day. Sally spoke to Emma on the telephone and sounded very excited.

She told Emma that it was the first time she had ever been visiting on her own and she was looking forward to it more than anything in the world. She felt like a real grown-up.

In the morning, Emma told Sheltie that they were having a tea party with Sally. She waggled a packet of peppermints in front of him.

'And you can have some of these if you behave.'

Sheltie snatched the packet out of Emma's hand and stood there with it sticking out of his mouth.

'Don't you *dare*!' said Emma with a half laugh.

Sheltie dropped the mints. As Emma bent down to pick them up Sheltie nudged her bottom with his muzzle and sent her flying. Then he galloped off and Emma chased him all around the paddock.

Mr Jones brought Sally over for tea at three o'clock on the dot. He kissed Sally goodbye and said he would be back at six to collect her.

Emma's mum told him not to worry and said she would take good care of Sally. They all stood and waved as Mr Jones drove off back down the lane.

It was a lovely sunny day, so Mum put a little table outside in the garden down by the paddock. Sheltie stood with his fuzzy chin resting on the top bar of the wooden fence, looking at all the sandwiches and little cakes. He knew that if he stood there watching long enough, Emma would give him a piece of carrot cake, and maybe a peppermint or two. Sheltie loved his peppermints.

Little Joshua and Mum sat at the table with Emma and Sally. It was so nice sitting out in the garden, and Sheltie entertained them with his clowning.

First, Sheltie galloped round in

circles. Then he rolled over on the grass kicking his legs up in the air as he lay on his back. And when he stood there and curled back his lips, showing two grinning rows of teeth, Sally laughed so much that she fell off her chair.

'I think Sheltie deserves a titbit,' said Mum. Joshua clapped his hands with glee.

Emma let Sally feed Sheltie a peppermint as a special treat.

While Sheltie was crunching away Emma asked Sally if she would like a ride.

Chapter Four

The two girls saddled up Sheltie and put on his bridle. Sheltie was smaller than Minnow, but Sally rode him beautifully. Sheltie was enjoying himself, and when Emma suggested a jump or two, his ears pricked up like a rabbit's.

Emma made the jump with bricks and the plank of wood. Six bricks high was easy for Sheltie now. So she made it eight. Then she rolled the wooden barrel out of the stable to make a little course of two jumps.

Sally rode Sheltie once around the paddock then took the first jump. After a short canter they went over the barrel. Everyone clapped and Sally blushed with pride.

'Do it again!' called Emma. Sally looked like a proper horsewoman. She really was a good little rider.

Sally took the jumps again. But as she circled the paddock to jump for a third time, she didn't see her father's car rolling down the lane and into the drive.

One . . . two! Sheltie cleared the jumps just as Mr Jones leaped out of the car.

'Sally!' he shouted at the top of his voice.

The loud noise surprised everyone and made them jump. Sheltie gave an unexpected hop and Sally slid sideways off the saddle. Sheltie stood still as Sally lay on the soft grass. She was unhurt.

Mr Jones came racing across to the paddock gate. He flung it open and ran to Sally. Emma got there first though and helped Sally up. Sally was perfectly all right, but Mr Jones was shouting and making a terrible fuss.

'I knew something like this would happen!' he said. 'I should never have let you come, Sally. You could have been killed!' He turned to

Emma's mum. His face was red and very angry.

'I thought you were going to look after her,' he said. 'I should have known better!' Then he took Sally's hand and led her quickly to the car.

Poor Sally started to cry and Sheltie, who thought he had done something terribly wrong, made a bolt for the open gate and ran off.

'Sheltie,' called Emma. 'Come back!' But Sheltie was gone, trotting down the lane.

Emma's mum followed Mr Jones to the car. 'Really, Mr Jones,' she said, 'there's no need to get upset. Sally has been having a lovely time. And there's no harm done.'

'Bah!' said Mr Jones. Then he

slammed the car door shut and drove
off.

Emma raced down the lane after
Sheltie. She found him waiting in Mr
Brown's meadow, hidden behind a
bush.

'Come on, boy,' said Emma. 'It's all

right. It wasn't your fault.' She rode
Sheltie back to the paddock.

'Oh dear,' said Mum. 'What a
shame. Sally was having such a nice
time as well!'

Emma's mum telephoned Fox Hall
Manor and spoke to Mrs Jones, who
said Sally was very upset and Mr
Jones had made her go to her room.
But Mrs Jones was very nice and told
Emma's mum not to worry. Her
husband would calm down and
everything would be all right in the
morning. He always fussed over
Sally and was a real worrier. She was
sorry that Sally's visit had ended the
way it did.

That night, Emma thought about
Sally a lot. She decided to write her

new friend a letter and take it round in the morning. There was a letter box in the big gates and Sally would be able to read it and cheer herself up. Emma thought it would be nice if Sally knew that she had a friend who was thinking about her.

Chapter Five

In the morning, after breakfast, when Emma and Sheltie rode up to the manor they found the gates wide open. There was no sign of Sally anywhere. Emma popped the letter into the box just as Mr Jones came out of the house.

He saw Emma and Sheltie standing by the gates and came racing down the drive. Mrs Jones followed right behind him.

'It's all your fault!' Mr Jones shouted at Emma. 'Sally's taken Minnow and run away. And it's all your fault, putting silly ideas of adventure into her head. My little girl's run away from home.'

Mrs Jones caught hold of her husband's arm.

'Don't say such things, Bernard,' she said. 'It's not Emma's fault at all. If it's anyone's fault then it's our own. Keeping Sally in all the time has made her run off, *not* Emma and Sheltie.'

Mr Jones calmed down a bit.

'But she's gone all the same. Sally's run away. Do you have any idea where she may have gone, Emma?' His voice sounded all croaky, as though he was about to burst into tears.

Emma shook her head. 'I'm sorry,' she said. 'I don't know where she could be. Perhaps she just went out for a little ride on her own. She told me she wanted to do that.'

'No, she's gone!' snapped Mr Jones. 'She left a note saying that she has run away and is never coming back.'

Sheltie put his head down. He didn't like it when people shouted.

'Maybe Sheltie and I can find Sally,' said Emma. 'We can go and look. We know all the bridle paths across the countryside and all around Little Applewood.'

'I can't see how your stupid pony

can find my little girl,' said Mr Jones.
'It's a job for the police. I telephoned
them half an hour ago. If anyone's
going to find her it will be the
police!'

Suddenly, Mrs Jones began crying.

'Oh, Bernard,' she said. 'Let Emma

go and look if she wants to. Sally is out there somewhere all on her own. We can't do anything here except wait.'

Mr Jones put his arm around his wife's shoulders and led her back inside the house. They were both very upset.

'Come on, Sheltie,' said Emma. 'Let's try and find Sally and Minnow.'

Sheltie pricked his ears up and gave a loud blow. He seemed to understand everything that Emma said.

Chapter Six

Emma squeezed her heels and Sheltie took off at a gallop. They raced down the lane to the woods behind Mr Brown's meadow. If Sally had run away, thought Emma, she would probably be heading for the open countryside, through the woods.

Emma and Sheltie took the path they always rode, the one which skirted the meadow to the woods.

Emma kept a lookout for any pony tracks. Sheltie sniffed at the air, trying to pick up Minnow's scent.

The ground was hard and Emma could see no marks to show that Sally and Minnow had passed that way.

Emma and Sheltie pressed on until they came to the edge of Bramble Wood. There were several paths which led through the tangle of trees.

Sheltie pawed at the ground with his hoof and tossed his head. He wanted to take the long path which led up to higher ground. From there you could look out over the hills and down across Little Applewood. The path went up over the downs towards the main road and led on to the rolling moor.

Emma and Sheltie rode through the woods beneath the overhanging trees. At some points, the branches hung so low that Emma had to brush them out of the way with her hand.

There was no sign of Sally though until they neared the edge of the wood where the path began to rise up to higher ground.

On a branch sticking out across the path, clinging to a twig, was a clump of white horse hair. Sheltie saw it first. He stopped dead in his tracks and sniffed at the coarse hair.

It was from Minnow's mane. Sheltie had no doubt about it. He recognized the scent right away.

Sheltie gave a loud snort as Emma
reached out with her hand and
plucked the clump of hair free.

'Clever boy, Sheltie,' said Emma.
'They must have come this way after
all.' There were also a few hoof prints
in the muddy track where the earth

was softer. Emma squeezed with her heels and hurried Sheltie along.

'Trot on, Sheltie!'

Sheltie quickened his pace to a trot. They rode out of the wood and climbed up to the top of the downs.

There weren't so many trees here. Emma could see for miles back down over Little Applewood and beyond, across to the rolling moor. There was still no sign of Sally and Minnow though.

'Which way, Sheltie?' said Emma.

Sheltie shook his long mane and sniffed the air through his nostrils. Minnow's scent was on the wind, but it was very faint.

Emma eased the reins and let Sheltie take the lead. He flicked his tail a couple of times. Then he set off over the grass across a shallow slope, heading for the moor.

An old railway line used to run through the valley on the other side of the slope between the moor and the downs. Emma could see where the railway tracks had been. The grass was thinner there and the ground was stony with gravel and rocks.

Emma and Sheltie followed the tracks until they disappeared into an abandoned tunnel that cut into the hillside. Sheltie stopped at the entrance to the tunnel and peered inside. A wooden barrier lay across the opening warning people to keep out. Sheltie made funny little

snorting sounds and pawed at the
ground with his hoof.

'Is it them, Sheltie?' said Emma.
'Are Sally and Minnow in there?'

Sheltie nodded his head and gave a
loud blow.

'Sally,' Emma called into the tunnel. 'Are you in there?'

Emma's voice echoed back from inside the tunnel.

'Are you in there . . . there . . . there.' The echo faded to silence. Then Emma heard someone calling. A little voice sounding far away.

'Help!'

Sheltie heard it too. His ears stood straight up.

'Sally, is that you?' Emma called again. And this time she recognized Sally's voice.

'Help! I'm in here!'

It was very dark inside the tunnel. But Emma knew Sally was in trouble, so she urged Sheltie forward.

Slowly they edged their way round

the barrier and into the darkness.
Sheltie had to be very careful. The
ground was uneven where the
railway tracks had been removed
and there were dips and holes
everywhere. Further into the
tunnel, the floor became wet and
slippery.

Emma saw a faint light up ahead.
It was Sally. She was walking back
along the tunnel towards Emma with
a torch. Sally carried a small
backpack and her clothes looked all
wet and muddy. Emma could see that
Sally had been crying. Her cheeks
were wet with tears.

'Sally!' called Emma.

Sally ran the last few metres to
meet her friend. Emma jumped down

from the saddle and gave poor Sally
a big hug.

'Oh, Emma,' cried Sally, 'I'm so
glad to see you! It's Minnow. He's
fallen down and trapped his leg. And
its all my fault.' She began to cry
again.

Chapter Seven

Sally told Emma how the ground suddenly sloped away down into a big dip up ahead. There was a hole where some old railway sleepers were stacked. Minnow had missed his footing and fallen into it. His leg was trapped by one of the wooden rails and he couldn't move. They could hear poor Minnow up ahead in the darkness, whimpering and making sad whinnying noises.

'We've got to help him,' said Sally. 'We've got to get Minnow out. I'll never run away again, I promise. I only wanted to ride out on my own like you and Sheltie, Emma. I never meant to put Minnow in danger.'

Emma held Sally's hand and led Sheltie along in the dark to where Minnow was trapped. Sally shone her torch and they could see the little black and white pony lying on his side in the hole, unable to get up.

Minnow's lovely white mane was all wet and muddy. He was very frightened. When Minnow saw Sheltie he calmed down a little and gave a friendly blow.

Emma climbed down the slope into the hole. The wooden rail was very heavy. As hard as Emma tried she couldn't move it. Minnow's leg was well and truly stuck.

'We need a rope,' said Emma. 'Then maybe Sheltie could help and pull the rail away.'

'But we haven't got a rope,' said Sally.

Emma thought about it for a while. Then she had an idea.

'We can use Minnow's reins,' she said. 'And I've got a belt. We can use the straps on your backpack and tie them all together.'

It was a brilliant idea and the two girls set to work without a moment to lose.

Sally climbed down to Minnow and carefully slipped the reins off over the little pony's head. Emma unclipped the two straps from Sally's backpack and took off the belt from her jeans.

When they tied them all together they had a strong line. It was long enough to fix around one end of the wooden rail that trapped Minnow's

leg. The other end was tied to
Sheltie's girth.

Emma turned Sheltie round. They
were ready to give it a try.

Emma gave Sheltie a hug and
whispered in his ear. 'It's up to you,
Sheltie. I know you can do it.'

She led Sheltie forward and the
line took the strain. Sheltie pulled as

hard as he could. The wooden rail
moved a little bit but not enough to
free Minnow's leg. A second rail was
stopping the first from moving any
further.

Sheltie tried again, but it was no
good. Each time Sheltie pulled, the
second rail seemed to stick even more.

'We mustn't give up,' said Sally.

'We've got to get Minnow out.'

Sheltie stood with his head cocked
to one side. Sally shone her torch into
the hole and Sheltie looked at the
problem.

Very slowly, Sheltie started to
move forward. Carefully, he picked
his way over the rails and went down
into the hole. Minnow raised his
head and the two ponies nuzzled
noses. Then Sheltie bent his head low
and began to push the second rail
with his nose.

Sheltie had a thick neck and was
very strong. The rail moved a little
bit. Then Sheltie pushed again and
nudged it to one side. One final push
and the rail came free and rolled
away. Minnow snorted.

Sheltie scrambled back up out of the hole and gave a loud snort. He was ready to try again and pull the other rail away.

Emma turned Sheltie around and led him forward again. This time the thick wooden rail moved easily.

As soon as Sheltie had dragged it free, Sally jumped down into the hole and helped Minnow up on to his feet. The little rescued pony was so happy to scramble out of the hole that he rushed up to Sheltie and gave a loud blow in his ear.

Emma clapped her hands with joy. The two girls untied the straps and reins, then unfastened the belt from Sheltie's girth. Sally put Minnow's reins back on to the bridle and put

her backpack together. As Emma
buckled up her belt the two girls
looked at each other with big smiles.
They had done it! Or rather, Sheltie
had.

Sally gave Sheltie a good hard pat.
She ruffled his mane and planted a
big kiss on his nose. Then she and
Emma led the two ponies back along
the tunnel.

Chapter Eight

'We must be very careful,' said Emma. 'There are still a lot of holes up ahead.'

They walked very slowly, one pony behind the other with Sheltie leading the way. They could see the light at the end of the tunnel. Soon they were all standing outside in the bright sunshine.

Minnow was limping slightly. His leg was grazed and very sore. 'He's going to have a nasty bruise there,' said Emma. 'You'll need to get the vet to come over and have a look at him, Sally.'

As they made their way back over the downs and along the woodland path, Sally looked worried.

'Daddy will be very cross,' she said. 'What with me running away and everything. And now Minnow's hurt. He's going to be *so* angry. I bet he won't let me ride Minnow ever again!'

Sally suddenly looked very sad.

'Don't be silly,' said Emma. 'He's going to be so pleased to see you safe and sound, he probably won't say anything.'

'Oh yes he will,' said Sally. 'You don't know him. It was wrong to run

away like that, but I just had to ride
Minnow out on my own. What's the
use of having a pony if you're not
allowed to ride him!'

'Perhaps he'll understand if you
explain,' said Emma.

'I hope so,' said Sally, but she knew
he wouldn't.

They finally came out of the wood
and took the curving path which
skirted the meadow and led to Fox
Hall Manor. Sally was shaking with
nerves.

The big manor house loomed up in
front of them. Emma and Sally walked
with the ponies side by side. Minnow
was still limping as they went through
the open gates and up to the house.

Suddenly the front door flew open

and Mr Jones came rushing out. Mrs Jones was right behind him. Her eyes were red from crying.

'Sally!' Mr Jones called out at the top of his voice. 'Where have you been?' He ran up to Sally and swept her up in his arms, pushing past Emma and accidentally knocking her off balance. Emma sat down with a bump.

Mrs Jones helped Emma up on to her feet.

'Thank heavens you're safe. Where on earth have you been? Why did you run off like that?'

Sally couldn't find her voice. She didn't say a thing.

'Sally only wanted to ride out on her own,' began Emma.

Mr Jones looked at her crossly. He was very angry.

'And what are *you* doing here?' he snapped. 'Go home! You've caused enough trouble for one day. This is all your fault. I never want to see you around here again!' Then he turned away and carried Sally up to the house.

Poor Emma was near to tears.

Mrs Jones took Minnow's rein and put a friendly hand on Emma's shoulder.

'I'm sorry about my husband, Emma,' said Mrs Jones. 'Don't take any notice. He's very upset. The police have been out for hours looking for Sally. I can't thank you enough for finding her and bringing her home. None of this is your fault, Emma.'

Emma swallowed back her tears. 'It was Sheltie really,' she said. 'Sheltie found Sally and Minnow. And he got Minnow out of the hole.'

Mrs Jones didn't know anything about the tunnel and how Minnow was trapped, but she suddenly noticed the pony's injured leg.

'I think you should call the vet,'

71

said Emma. 'Minnow's leg needs looking after.'

'Thank you, Emma. I'll telephone him straight away. Now you go home. Your mother will be getting worried.' She thanked Emma again then led Minnow off to his stable.

Emma and Sheltie watched her go, then closed the gates behind them and went home.

'You're just in time to help me lay out the plates for lunch,' said Mum. She popped some meat pies into the oven and took some knives and forks from the kitchen drawer.

When Emma didn't say anything, Mum noticed that she was upset. Something was wrong. Even little Joshua could tell that Emma was unhappy. He stopped scribbling in his drawing book and looked up.

'What's the matter, Emma?' asked Mum.

Emma told her everything that had happened. How Sally had run away and how Sheltie had led the way to the old railway tunnel where Minnow was trapped.

Mum listened carefully as Emma described how clever Sheltie had been and how they had made a line and rescued the little pony.

When she told Mum how cross Mr Jones had been, Mum understood why Emma was so upset.

'Oh dear, Emma. It must have been awful. But it wasn't your fault. Mr Jones must have been terribly worried all the same. You were very brave and clever to find Sally and Minnow like that. Good old Sheltie. It's a good job he's such a clever little pony.'

'But Mr Jones said I mustn't ever

see Sally again. It's not fair!' Emma started to cry and Mum gave her a cuddle.

'I expect he'll calm down now that Sally's safe and sound,' said Mum. 'Give him a day or two. I'm sure he'll see sense. He's probably very sorry for all those things he said.'

But Emma wondered if Mr Jones ever would see sense. He had looked so angry. Emma thought he would never forgive her for what had happened, even though it wasn't her fault at all.

Chapter Nine

All that afternoon, Emma kept thinking about poor Sally. She tried to imagine what it would be like if she could never ride Sheltie outside in the beautiful countryside. Emma felt very lucky but very sad and sorry for Sally at the same time.

Emma spent the rest of the afternoon in the paddock with Sheltie. She kept herself busy, mucking out his field shelter and polishing his saddle and bridle.

Then she gave Sheltie a good brush and groomed his tail and mane until it was time to go in for tea. Sheltie had never looked so neat and tidy. He would never look as smart as Minnow, but Emma loved him the way he was.

After tea, Emma thought about riding over to Fox Hall Manor just to see if she could catch a glimpse of Sally. But Mum said it would be best to keep away for a while and give Mr Jones time to calm down. Mum said that she would telephone Mrs Jones in the morning and ask after Sally.

That evening Emma watched her favourite programme on television before she went to bed, but all the time she kept thinking of poor Sally. At least she would be able to see Sally when she started school, she thought. That cheered her up. Mr Jones couldn't stop Sally from going to school.

In the morning, while Emma was out giving Sheltie his breakfast, Mum telephoned Mrs Jones. Mum told Emma that Mr Jones was coming over later to have a talk.

Emma was worried when she heard this, so Mum suggested that Emma took a picnic lunch up to Horseshoe Pond to keep out of the way. Emma didn't argue.

Mum made up a little basket of goodies, with sandwiches, cakes,

crisps and a big bottle of orangeade.
There was so much food in the basket
Emma thought that she would never
manage to eat it all on her own.

Sheltie was very interested in the
picnic basket. He could smell the

sandwiches and cakes, and tried to pull out a packet of crisps as Emma laid the basket down on the grass to saddle him up.

'Not yet, Sheltie. There will be plenty for you when we get to Horseshoe Pond,' said Emma.

Sheltie could hardly wait. He became frisky, and swished his tail with excitement.

They took the long way round through the apple orchard and followed the little stream to the big meadow. Emma popped two apples into the basket for Sheltie.

'Wouldn't it have been nice, Sheltie, if Sally could have come?' said Emma. Sheltie twitched his ears and listened as Emma spoke.

Horseshoe Pond was as pretty as ever. Emma sat on the little island. Sheltie nibbled at the dandelions growing beneath the sycamore tree as Emma fed the ducks on the pond with one of the cakes from the picnic basket.

Suddenly, Sheltie looked up, bright and alert. His eyes shone through his long fringe as he sniffed the air.

Then Sheltie gave a loud snort and Emma looked round. Trotting across the meadow on Minnow was Sally!

Emma jumped up. She couldn't believe it. At first she thought Sally had run away again. But then she saw that Sally was laughing and smiling with a big cheeky grin.

Sheltie did a funny little stomping
dance and ran forward to greet
Minnow.

'What are you doing here?' said
Emma. 'Your dad will go mad!'

'No, he won't,' laughed Sally as
she leaped from the saddle. 'I think

everything's going to be all right after all. Mummy had a long talk with Daddy this morning. And now he's at the cottage talking with *your* mum and dad. He's finally agreed to let me ride out on my own. Mummy says I'm old enough to keep out of trouble. Daddy didn't like the idea very much. But he said I can as long as I promised not to go too far. Isn't it fantastic?'

Emma was so pleased.

'Did my mum send you over here?' asked Emma.

'Yes,' laughed Sally. 'She spoke to Mummy this morning and asked about the picnic.'

Emma suddenly realized why there was so much food in the picnic basket. Her mum had known all along that Sally would be able to come. It was the best surprise ever.

The two girls sat beneath the sycamore tree and laid out all the

sandwiches and cakes on the picnic cloth. Sheltie and Minnow nuzzled up to each other and stood quietly in the shade, nibbling grass.

From the little island, Emma pointed out to Sally all the best places to ride. Sally couldn't wait to explore. It was going to be brilliant living in Little Applewood and having Emma and Sheltie as her friends.

A little while later, Mr Jones came walking by with Emma's mum and dad. Joshua was riding piggyback on Dad's shoulders.

Mr Jones was smiling and Emma thought he looked really nice. Much better than the grumpy man he was before. He apologized to Emma and told her how sorry he was for being so rude.

'I've been a very silly man,' he said. 'Ever since my friend's little girl was hurt I've worried about Sally being hurt too. But accidents can happen anywhere. And it can't be much fun having a pony with nowhere to ride it.'

He really was very grateful to Emma and Sheltie for finding Sally and bringing her home safely.

'You're a very brave and clever girl, Emma,' said Mr Jones. 'And Sheltie must be the cleverest pony for miles around.'

And with that, Sheltie snatched a packet of crisps from Emma's hand

and raced off across the meadow
with Minnow giving chase.

Mr Jones laughed with a loud
bellow.

'I can see Sally's going to be in safe
hands with friends like Emma and
Sheltie to look out for her,' he said.

Sheltie Finds
a Friend

For Dorothy, Tony,
Sarah, and Miles

Chapter One

It was a lovely spring day in Little
Applewood. Emma was in the
paddock with Sheltie. They were
playing Frisbee. Emma was trying
to teach the little Shetland pony
to catch the saucer-shaped
disc.

Sheltie was a clever pony and
enjoyed every minute of this new
game. He wasn't very good at it

though. He couldn't catch for all the tea in China.

Emma threw the frisbee and watched it sail through the air. The disc landed at Sheltie's feet and the little Shetland pony gave a loud snort. He shook his long shaggy mane.

Sheltie bent his head and picked up the frisbee between his teeth. Then, with a sudden flick, he tossed the plastic saucer up into the air.

Little Joshua was sitting on the paddock fence with Mum, watching the game. He clapped his hands together as Sheltie sent the frisbee spinning over his head.

'Sheltie must be the only pony in the world who can do that,' said Mum.

Emma took a packet of peppermints
from her jacket pocket and gave
Sheltie one of his favourite treats.

'He's not very good at catching
though,' said Emma. But it didn't
matter. Sheltie was a pony, not a
person. And Emma laughed each time

he picked up the frisbee and tossed it
backwards over his head.

The very next morning there was a
surprise waiting for Emma down in
the paddock.

Every day, the first thing Emma
did when she woke up was to look at
Sheltie out of her bedroom window.
This morning when Emma looked,
she could hardly believe her eyes.

As usual, Sheltie was standing by
the paddock gate with his fuzzy chin
resting on the top bar of the wooden
fence. But standing there right next to
him was a little black donkey.

Emma rubbed her eyes and looked
again.

'Where did *he* come from?' said

94

Emma. She pulled on her school uniform and hurried downstairs.

Mum and Dad were already sitting at the breakfast table. They were both wearing huge grins.

'Have you seen the donkey, Emma?' said Dad. 'His name is Mudlark.'

'Who does he belong to?' asked Emma. She couldn't wait to rush out to the paddock for a closer look.

Chapter Two

The little black donkey was almost the same size as Sheltie. But not quite so fat.

They stood side by side in the paddock, looking over the fence and up into the garden. When the donkey saw Emma he threw back his head and brayed with a loud hee-haw.

Emma laughed and reached over to

stroke Mudlark's furry head. His
mane felt very bristly.

Sheltie gave a snort and nudged
the donkey with his soft muzzle.
Mudlark gave another bray and his
long ears waggled like a big rabbit's.

'Isn't he funny?' said Mum. She
picked Joshua up so that he could see
better.

'Do you remember us telling you
about Marjorie Wallace, Emma?' said
Dad. 'She's the old lady who lives in
the cottage at the foot of Beacon Hill.'

Emma remembered. Marjorie
Wallace had nine cats. She took in
strays and found homes for
unwanted kittens.

'Well, Mudlark belongs to
Marjorie,' said Mum. 'The poor old

lady hasn't had a holiday for ages.
She doesn't like to leave her cats and
never goes anywhere outside the
village.'

'Marjorie has a sister,' said Dad.

'And a brother somewhere,' said
Mum.

'Yes, but nobody knows much
about him,' said Dad. 'Anyway,
Marjorie hasn't seen her sister for six
years. So all her friends in Little
Applewood thought it would be a
good idea if Marjorie went for a visit.
And we're helping out by looking
after Mudlark while she's away.'

Emma thought this was a
wonderful idea. And Sheltie thought
it was fun too. He blew a raspberry
and gave Mudlark a gentle push.

The little donkey brayed, then galloped around the paddock. Sheltie was close at his heels, playing chase.

'Who will be looking after Marjorie's cats?' asked Emma.

'Mrs Marsh is staying at the cottage while Marjorie's away. And the gardener said he would pop in from time to time to make sure everything is all right.

'One of Marjorie's cats has kittens, Emma. We thought you and Sheltie might like to ride over there after school to see them.'

'Oh, yes please,' said Emma.

Joshua started to wriggle in Mum's arms. He wanted to go and see the kittens too.

Emma unlocked the paddock gate and gave Sheltie and Mudlark their breakfast. Dad had put a bucket in Sheltie's field shelter for Mudlark. The bucket was pushed tightly into an old car tyre so that it wouldn't get kicked over.

Emma stood back and watched Sheltie and Mudlark feeding. They both gobbled their breakfast down in seconds.

Next, Emma filled the water trough with the hose. Mudlark blew bubbles in the water. Emma gave him a squirt and Mudlark threw back his head with a loud hee-haw. Sheltie answered with a loud snort and chased him across the paddock.

'I don't know which one is worse,'

laughed Mum. 'Sheltie or Mudlark. I
can see you're going to have your
hands full this week, Emma!'

Chapter Three

After school, Emma rode Sheltie over to Marjorie Wallace's cottage at Beacon Hill. Emma was looking forward to seeing the kittens.

The cottage nestled at the foot of the hill, which was on the outskirts of the village.

As Sheltie trotted along towards the cottage, Emma saw someone hop over Marjorie's low garden wall.

She had never seen this man before. He was quite old, dressed in rough-looking clothes and was carrying a sack. Emma was too far away to see him properly, but she watched as he disappeared into the woods behind the cottage. Perhaps it was the gardener, she thought.

Emma dismounted and led Sheltie through the garden gate and up the path to the front door.

There was a big metal ring in the cottage wall. Emma tied Sheltie's rein to the ring and knocked on the red painted door.

Emma waited but nobody came. She knocked again, louder this time, and heard footsteps inside. The cottage door swung open and

Mrs Marsh stood on the front step.

'Hello,' said Emma. 'I've come to see the kittens.' She gave Mrs Marsh her biggest smile.

'Oh dear,' said Mrs Marsh. 'You had better come in, Emma. You see, one of the kittens has gone missing. I can't find it anywhere. Perhaps you can help me find it.'

Emma hunted high and low, all over the cottage. She looked in all the places she could think of where a kitten might hide.

She even looked outside, but there was no sign of the kitten anywhere.

'Perhaps it wandered off to explore,' she said. 'It'll come back when it's hungry. Cats always do.'

'But it's so tiny,' said Mrs Marsh. 'I

can't think where it could have gone.'

Emma stayed for half an hour and played with the other kittens. But when it was time to leave there was still no sign of the missing one.

As Emma and Sheltie rode away, Emma suddenly remembered the old man with the sack – the man she had seen hop over the garden wall and disappear into the woods.

I wonder what he had in that sack, thought Emma. Perhaps it was the kitten!

*

Back in the paddock, Dad was busy fitting Mudlark with a special harness. Emma's eyes grew wide as she watched Dad wheel a funny little cart out from behind Sheltie's field shelter.

Sheltie gave a loud snort and Mudlark answered with an even louder hee-haw.

'What's that for?' asked Emma. She jumped out of the saddle to take a better look.

The little cart was painted in bright colours, with swirly patterns. It had two big wheels, and a little seat at the front. Two long shafts fitted perfectly into Mudlark's harness. The cart looked like a small pony trap.

'It's Mudlark's fish cart,' said Dad. 'Before Marjorie adopted Mudlark he belonged to her brother, who used to sell and deliver fresh fish to the houses in the village. That was years ago, before her brother went off, but Marjorie still uses the cart to collect her weekly shopping. Mudlark loves to pull it along and give rides, don't you, Mudlark?'

The little black donkey replied with a loud hee-haw.

'Would you like a ride, Emma?' said Dad.

'Oh, yes please,' said Emma. But first she took Sheltie's saddle off and slipped the bridle over his head. She lay them carefully over the top bar of the fence, then climbed into the cart.

Mum came out of the cottage with Joshua, to watch.

Emma took Mudlark's long reins and Dad led the donkey around the paddock. Sheltie thought this was great fun and trotted alongside. He tossed his head and swatted Emma with his swishing tail.

Once Emma was used to the reins, Dad let go and Emma drove the little fish cart around the paddock on her own, in a big circle.

Then Joshua wanted a ride. So Mum lifted him on to the seat next to Emma and Mudlark pulled them both along. Joshua gurgled with laughter as the little cart trundled around the paddock.

When the ride was over, Mum took Joshua inside and put a pizza in the oven for their tea.

Dad took Mudlark out of the
harness and wheeled the cart back
behind Sheltie's field shelter. Then he
went into the cottage to help Mum.

Chapter Four

Emma stayed in the paddock for a
while with Sheltie. She was about to put
his saddle and bridle away when she
noticed a man standing by the fence
talking to Mudlark. The man was
scratching Mudlark's ears and the
donkey was enjoying every minute of it.

The man looked like the old
gardener that Emma had seen earlier
at Marjorie's cottage.

'Good afternoon, miss,' said the man politely. 'That's a fine donkey you have there. I could use a donkey like that.'

Emma thought that was a funny thing to say. She pulled a face and said, 'He doesn't belong to us. We're

only looking after him for Marjorie Wallace while she's away.'

'Oh,' said the man with a smile. Then he touched his cap politely and said goodbye.

Emma watched the man walk away up the lane. Although she had never seen him before, Emma thought that the man looked very familiar. He reminded her of someone, but she couldn't think who.

Emma quickly put Sheltie's tack away, then rushed inside to tell Mum and Dad.

'It doesn't sound like Mr Rudd, the gardener,' said Dad. 'Perhaps it was the new hired help at Mr Brown's place. He has a workman doing some odd jobs around the farm.'

'Well, I didn't like him,' said Emma. 'He wanted Mudlark.'

'He was probably just being friendly,' said Mum.

Dad put some pizza slices on to plates and Mum carried them to the kitchen table. They all sat down to eat.

Later that evening, when Emma went up to bed, she lay awake thinking about the missing kitten. Emma wondered if Mrs Marsh had found it yet. She decided to ride over again first thing in the morning and find out.

But the next morning Emma made a terrible discovery. When she went to the paddock Mudlark was nowhere to be seen.

The paddock gate was locked and bolted and there were no breaks in the fence or any holes where the donkey could have escaped. But Mudlark had gone. Emma ran back inside to fetch Mum. Mum could hardly believe it. She went outside to see for herself.

Sheltie was tossing his head and dashing around the paddock.

'Do you know what happened, Sheltie?' said Mum. 'Where's Mudlark gone?'

Sheltie stared up into the branches of an overhanging tree. He gave a loud snort and scraped at the grass with his hoof.

Emma glanced up into the tree and saw a man's flat cap hanging from one of the branches.

'How did that get up there?' said
Emma.

Mum went to fetch a broom. Then
she reached up into the tree and
knocked the cap off the branch.

When the cap fell to the ground
Sheltie rushed over and picked it up
between his teeth. Then with a quick
flick, he tossed it up into the air, just
like a frisbee.

'Did you throw it up there before, Sheltie?' said Mum.

'I think he must have,' said Emma. 'I bet whoever's taken Mudlark dropped it, and Sheltie tossed it up into the tree.'

'We'd better tell Dad and call the police,' said Mum.

Chapter Five

Half an hour later PC Green arrived on his bicycle. He examined the padlock and chain, and the bolt on the paddock gate, then scratched his head.

'And you say there's no trace of the donkey anywhere?'

Dad shook his head. 'We've looked everywhere,'

'And called him,' said Mum. 'He's definitely gone.'

'Stolen,' said Emma. 'Someone's stolen him! I bet it was that man.'

'We can't be sure of that yet, Emma,' said the policeman.

He looked around the paddock again, checking the fence. But there were no clues to Mudlark's disappearance. Then Mum handed over the cap.

'We found this,' she said. It was an ordinary brown checked cap.

'This could belong to anyone,' said the policeman.

'I bet it belongs to the thief,' said Emma.

'I shall report the incident and organize a search,' said the policeman. 'But I expect, if your donkey *has* been stolen, then he's miles away by now.'

'Oh dear,' said Mum. 'Whatever shall we tell poor Marjorie!'

PC Green looked out in the lane for fresh tyre tracks. But there were none. The weather had been fine for weeks, and the lane was dry and dusty.

There were no footprints either. No hoof marks. No tyre tracks. No clues at all. And no Mudlark.

'Sheltie must have seen who took Mudlark,' said Emma.

PC Green smiled. 'But I'm afraid Sheltie can't tell us, can he, Emma?'

I bet he can, thought Emma. But she didn't say so.

When the policeman left to organize a search, Emma took another look around the paddock.

Mum and Dad went back inside

the cottage. Mum looked very worried. Dad thought it was best not to telephone Marjorie just yet. He didn't want to spoil her holiday. He said they should wait a while and see if the police found Mudlark.

Out in the paddock, Sheltie was nosing about in the long grass by the gatepost. He pawed at the earth and kept pushing his muzzle into a clump of nettles which grew there.

Emma went over to see what Sheltie was so interested in.

Sheltie pushed his head forward into the long grass and gave a loud sneeze. Emma carefully parted the nettles. She found a tiny scrap of red woollen cloth caught on a bramble by the gatepost.

The scrap was no bigger than a
postage stamp. Emma took the bit of
wool in to show Mum and Dad.

'It could be a piece of jumper or a
scarf,' said Mum. 'But none of us has
anything that colour. It's probably
been there for ages, Emma.'

But Emma didn't think so. She was
certain that Sheltie didn't either. They
both thought it was a clue.

Emma put the red woolly scrap into her back pocket.

'I hope the policemen find Mudlark soon,' said Emma. 'What would the thieves do with him?'

'Well, he could end up anywhere,' said Dad. 'Probably in a market somewhere, to be sold as a working donkey.'

'Oh, poor Mudlark,' said Emma. 'How awful. He's far too old to work. And he'll miss Marjorie.' She was close to tears. And she kept thinking how horrible it would be if Sheltie had been stolen.

Chapter Six

When Dad came home from work,
everyone was sitting around the
kitchen table. Emma and Joshua were
drawing. All day at school Emma had
thought about poor Mudlark. So far
she had drawn eight pictures. They
were all of donkeys.

Dad telephoned the police station.
They told him that their search had
found nothing. They had even been

over to Mr Brown's farm to question
the new workman. But the workman
had finished all the odd jobs around
the place. He had even mended the
old rusty lock on the cowshed. Mr
Brown had paid him his wages and
he had already gone on his way.

After tea, Emma decided to ride
Sheltie over to Beacon Hill to visit Mrs
Marsh again. She was hoping that the
kitten had turned up. But there was no
such luck.

'I've been searching and searching,'
said Mrs Marsh. 'And I still can't find
it. It's disappeared.'

'Or been stolen,' said Emma. She
told Mrs Marsh about Mudlark and
the man she had seen hopping over

the garden wall the previous day.

'It couldn't have been Mr Rudd, the gardener. He's not due until tomorrow,' said Mrs Marsh. They both looked puzzled.

'I bet it was that man then,' said Emma. 'And I bet he's taken Mudlark *and* the kitten.'

Mrs Marsh didn't know what to think.

When Emma had to leave, she climbed into Sheltie's saddle and squeezed with her heels.

'Trot on, Sheltie. Trot on.' And Sheltie trotted off. But he wouldn't go the way Emma wanted him to.

Sheltie turned around and went up the path towards the woods behind Marjorie's cottage.

Emma let Sheltie take the lead. They trotted along the path and into the woods.

Emma knew that Sheltie wanted to show her something. He kept his head high and sniffed at the wind as he went along.

A little way into the woods they came to a clearing. Up ahead, sheltered by some overhanging trees, Emma saw a funny-looking caravan.

The caravan was tiny. It looked like a little garden shed on wheels.

Near by, tied to a tree, were two donkeys. One donkey was grey and the other one was almost pure white. It looked like a ghost.

Sheltie sniffed at the air and both his ears pricked up.

Emma slipped out of the saddle.
She and Sheltie were hidden from
view by a thicket of shrubs. They
kept very quiet and watched as an
old man came out of the caravan.

It was the same man that Emma
had seen hopping over Marjorie's
garden wall. And the same man who

had spoken to her in the paddock. Emma was certain of it.

He did remind her of someone. But Emma *still* couldn't think who.

She held her breath and watched as the man untied the white donkey and led it away, off into the woods.

When he had gone, Emma crept out from her hiding place. Sheltie gave a snort and watched her tiptoe towards the caravan.

Behind the caravan, Emma found a washing line strung out across two poles.

On the line was a shirt, a vest and a pair of red socks. Emma stared at the socks. Her eyes grew wide and her heart thumped in her chest.

The socks were the same colour as

the scrap of woolly material that
Sheltie had found by the paddock
gate.

Emma took a closer look at the
socks. And there, in one of them, was
a tear. A hole no bigger than a
postage stamp.

Emma took the woolly scrap out of
her pocket and held it up against the
sock. The colour matched perfectly.
That meant that the man who owned

the socks had been in the paddock. And he must have stolen Mudlark!

As Emma stood by the caravan she thought she heard a cat miaow. Emma listened carefully and pressed her ear against the painted wood. She heard the miaow again. The sound was coming from inside the caravan.

Suddenly, a twig snapped in the woods. Emma jumped. The man was coming back. Sheltie gave a warning blow and Emma ran back and jumped into the saddle.

She squeezed her heels and Sheltie took off, trotting back through the woods and along the path to Beacon Hill.

Chapter Seven

Emma decided to ride straight back home and tell Mum and Dad what she had discovered.

When she burst in through the kitchen door, Emma was red in the face and out of breath.

She told Mum and Dad all about the funny little caravan in the woods, the socks on the washing line and the cat crying.

When she had finished, Dad reached for the telephone to call PC Green at the station again.

The policeman went to the woods behind Beacon Hill straight away. But when he got there the caravan had gone. There was no sign of it anywhere. No Mudlark and no tracks on the leafy forest floor.

Everyone was very disappointed.

'Perhaps we should telephone Marjorie at her sister's and tell her what's happening,' said Mum.

PC Green thought they should wait a little while longer. The next day was Saturday and there would be three markets in neighbouring villages. Maybe Mudlark would be put up for sale at one of them. PC

Green suggested waiting to see what happened.

'There's no point in causing unnecessary worry,' he said. They all agreed.

'The markets start early in the morning, so we should know by midday if the thief is going to try to sell the little donkey.'

That night, when she went to bed, Emma lay awake thinking about poor Mudlark. She wondered where he was and kept thinking how sad and frightened he must be and how awful it would be for Marjorie when she found out that her donkey had been stolen.

When Emma finally went off to

sleep she had a bad dream. She dreamed that Sheltie had been stolen and she was running all over Little Applewood looking for him. But she couldn't find him anywhere.

In the morning, Emma woke suddenly and jumped out of bed. She ran over to look out of her bedroom window and breathed a sigh of relief. Sheltie was out there in the paddock as usual, looking over the wooden fence.

Everyone was very quiet during breakfast. Emma wasn't hungry at all

and pushed her cereal around in the bowl with her spoon.

All they could do was wait and see if Mudlark turned up at any of the markets.

Chapter Eight

At twelve o'clock, PC Green came to the cottage. There was still no news of Mudlark. He hadn't been spotted at any one of the three markets.

'I'm afraid there's not much hope of finding him now,' said the policeman. 'Perhaps you should contact Mrs Wallace after all.'

Mum tried to telephone Marjorie, but there was no reply.

'They must have gone out,' she said. 'I'll try again later.'

Emma thought she would take Sheltie out for a ride over to Beacon Hill again. She wanted to call in on Mrs Marsh to see if the missing kitten had found its way home. Emma kept thinking about the miaowing she had heard from inside the caravan. She was almost certain that it was the kitten.

Emma talked to Sheltie as she plopped the saddle on to his back.

'Do you know where Mudlark is, Sheltie?'

Sheltie tilted his head to one side, listening.

As Emma strapped the leather girth under his fat tummy, she said, 'I bet if anyone can find Mudlark, you can.'

By the time she had fitted the bridle and sat up in the saddle holding the reins, Sheltie was eager to set off.

Emma rode Sheltie out of the paddock and squeezed her heels to send him trotting down the lane.

But Sheltie didn't want to go that way and headed off in the opposite direction. Emma let the reins go slack and Sheltie took the lead.

'Are we going to find Mudlark, Sheltie?' asked Emma. Sheltie blew from his nostrils and quickened his pace.

They crossed Mr Brown's meadow, and rode past Horseshoe Pond to the back field. There Bramble Woods began and swept back in a wide arc all the way across to Beacon Hill. The woods were much thicker at that end, and led off, up and over the hills, on to the open downs and beyond.

Sheltie carried on, following the bridle path into the woods. They both knew that track very well. Emma knew that the thickest part of the wood lay up ahead.

As they climbed the rise, Emma looked back and saw Mr Brown's farm nestling in the fields below. It was the perfect spot for looking out across the countryside and the whole of Little Applewood.

As they reached the top the trees grew thicker and the ground levelled

out. Sheltie left the track and headed
into the deepest part of the wood.

They hadn't gone far when Emma
gasped. Up ahead, nestling beneath
the trees, was the little caravan. Two
donkeys were harnessed to the
caravan's shafts. The grey one and

the ghostly white one.

Sheltie stopped and Emma slid out of the saddle. Sheltie let out an excited snort. 'Shh,' whispered Emma. She pressed a finger to her lips.

They hid behind a big bush and watched. There was no sign of anyone.

Then Emma heard someone whistling and she saw the old man stepping out of the caravan. He was walking straight towards them. Emma held her breath and whispered to Sheltie to keep still.

Chapter Nine

The man walked straight past them, just ten metres away. He carried on whistling and followed the track down the hill through the woods. He was carrying an empty plastic container. Emma guessed that he was heading for the stream to fetch some water.

Emma and Sheltie watched the man disappear through the trees.

When it was safe to come out of hiding, Emma left the bush and approached the caravan. Sheltie gave a snort and followed.

As soon as the ghostly white donkey saw Emma and Sheltie it threw back its head with a loud hee-haw, just like Mudlark.

Sheltie rushed over and nuzzled the white donkey with his nose as though he were greeting a long-lost friend. The donkey's long ears stood straight up and Sheltie began licking them.

Emma watched as the donkey's ears turned from white to black. Suddenly Emma realized that it *was* Mudlark. He had been covered from head to hoof with white flour!

Emma looked around and wondered what to do next. Then she heard a miaow. It's the kitten, she thought.

The sound was coming from inside the caravan. Emma reached for the caravan door and gave the handle a turn. The little door swung open and Emma stepped inside.

The caravan was very small and

very untidy. There were clothes thrown everywhere, a jumble of old newspapers, and things packed in cardboard boxes. Emma saw a brown checked jacket scrunched up in a ball on the low bunk bed. It was the same colour and pattern as the cap which Sheltie had tossed into the tree.

Curled up in the middle of the jacket was an old grey tabby cat. Not the missing kitten after all. The cat opened one lazy green eye and miaowed.

Outside, Sheltie was becoming very agitated. He gave a snort and scraped at the ground with his hoof. He was shaking his head and blowing loudly.

The man was coming back. Emma

peered through the only window at the rear of the caravan and saw him walking back up the track.

It was too late to run. The man would see her. Clever Sheltie had gone deeper into the woods and was standing behind a clump of bushes. Emma pulled the caravan door closed and stayed inside. She quickly looked around for somewhere to hide.

Suddenly, she noticed a space under the bed and crawled into it.

The caravan door opened and the old man stepped inside. He sat down on the bunk and the bed springs groaned, centimetres above Emma's head.

Emma could see the man's feet and legs in front of her. He was wearing

the red socks, the ones with the hole
in them. Emma could see the hole
quite clearly. It was just above his
shoe. Her heart beat faster and faster.

Chapter Ten

A few minutes passed by. It seemed like hours. The man was talking to the cat, which was purring loudly.

'What a pity we missed Marji, Tigger! Never mind. Maybe we'll see her next time we're passing through. I hope Marji doesn't mind too much about Mudlark. I felt mean taking him like that, but those nice people would never have just handed him over.'

Then the man got up and went outside. He locked the door behind him and Emma heard him climb up into the driving seat at the front of the caravan.

She heard a jangling of reins and the man called out 'Giddy-up!' The caravan rolled forward slowly and bumped across the uneven ground, with Emma inside.

Emma crawled out from under the bed. She peered out of the window and saw Sheltie peeping from behind the thicket, watching as the caravan pulled away.

The caravan was heading up to the open downs and would cross the moor to join the main road.

Sheltie gave a snort and flicked his

tail. Emma didn't know what to do.
She looked at Sheltie and waved her
hands. Get help, Sheltie, she thought.
Go and fetch help. And Sheltie
turned and galloped away, just as
though he had understood.

Sheltie was a very clever pony. He
knew that Emma was in trouble. He

wanted to follow the caravan, but it might be better to bring help.

Sheltie galloped as fast as he could, crashing through the woods along the bridle path back down to Little Applewood.

Sheltie knew the path very well. Every dip and turn. His little legs covered the distance quickly.

Sheltie headed for home. He crossed Mr Brown's meadow and was soon galloping up the lane to the cottage.

Mum and Dad were in the kitchen with Joshua, talking about Marjorie and poor Mudlark. They still hadn't been able to reach her by telephone.

Sheltie came trotting in through the open kitchen door. His hooves clattered on the polished floor tiles.

Mum jumped up out of her chair
with a fright. Joshua giggled as Dad
caught hold of Sheltie's reins.

'Whoa, Sheltie,' said Dad. 'Where's
Emma?'

Mum took Sheltie outside to see if
Emma was in the paddock. Sometimes
Sheltie slipped away from Emma just

for fun. Dad came outside with
Joshua. They saw that Emma was
nowhere around. Dad called her.

'Emma! Emma!'

There was no reply.

'Something must have happened,'
said Mum.

'Emma told me she was going over
to visit Mrs Marsh. I'll give her a
ring.' Mum hurried inside and picked
up the telephone.

Mrs Marsh said she hadn't seen
Emma all day. But she told Mum that
she would walk the footpath to the
top of Beacon Hill and look for her.
You could see for miles up there.

Outside, Sheltie was getting
impatient. He stamped the ground
with his feet and shook his mane.

Then he ran off a little way towards
the paddock and stopped, looking
back at Mum and Dad standing
outside the cottage.

'He wants us to follow him,' said
Mum.

Sheltie trotted into the paddock
and disappeared behind his field
shelter. When Mum and Dad got
there, Sheltie was standing between

the shafts of Mudlark's little fish cart. He was blowing and snorting like mad.

'I think he wants you to go with him in the cart,' said Mum. They both knew that Sheltie was trying to help.

Chapter Eleven

Dad quickly slipped Mudlark's
special harness over Sheltie and fitted
the shafts of the fish cart in place.

'Let Sheltie take you to Emma,'
said Mum. 'I'll stay here with Joshua
and telephone the police.'

'But how will you know where we
are heading?' said Dad.

'I'll watch and see which way you
go,' said Mum.

Dad jumped into the fish cart and Sheltie was off. Mum watched as Sheltie pulled the cart out of the paddock, down the lane and across Mr Brown's meadow, heading for the back field and Bramble Woods.

Sheltie was only a little Shetland pony but he was very strong for his size. He pulled the fish cart all the way up the rise where the trees grew thicker and the ground levelled out.

Sheltie didn't stop once. He pulled the cart along the track through the woods and out on to the edge of the downs.

A high ridge swept around and across to Beacon Hill. Mrs Marsh was up there looking for Emma. She stood by the side of the track as

Sheltie trotted up with Dad in the cart.

Mrs Marsh looked surprised.

'Any sign of Emma?' asked Dad.

'I'm afraid not,' said Mrs Marsh. 'But I saw a funny little caravan a moment ago, crossing the clearing over there.' She pointed towards a low rolling slope a short distance away.

'Two donkeys pulling a little caravan,' she said. 'Only minutes ago. It must be heading for the main road.'

The little fish cart flew along. Sheltie galloped as fast as his legs could carry him. The cart bumped down the rolling slope and on to the downs.

Up ahead, they could see the
caravan and the grey tarmac road
beyond. As they drew nearer Dad
suddenly saw Emma peering out
through the caravan window. He was
so surprised that he stood up . . . and
fell out of the cart. He landed on the
grass with a bump, but he was
unhurt.

Sheltie looked back, but he didn't

stop. He could go faster now without Dad's weight in the cart, so he galloped on and soon he was level with the caravan.

The driver was very surprised to see a Shetland pony appear out of nowhere. And even more surprised when Sheltie overtook the two donkeys and stopped suddenly in front of the moving caravan.

The donkeys stopped dead in their tracks and the caravan came to a sudden halt.

The old man jangled the reins and yelled, 'Giddy-up, Mudlark, Sophie.' But the donkeys didn't move. Instead, Mudlark just threw back his head and gave a loud hee-haw!

Chapter Twelve

Everything seemed to happen at once. A police car came roaring down the main road. Mum had told the police that Sheltie was heading in that direction. The police car screeched to a halt when the caravan had been spotted. PC Green jumped out.

Dad was also on his feet and ran up alongside. He pulled open the caravan door and Emma stepped out.

The man just sat there holding the limp reins.

'Where on earth did *she* come from?' He could hardly believe his own eyes. He suddenly looked very worried.

Emma ran into Dad's arms.

'I think you've got some explaining to do,' said PC Green.

'Oh dear,' said the man. 'I never meant any harm. I had no idea that the little girl was inside.' The old man was very confused.

'It's true,' said Emma. 'He didn't know I was in there.' Emma thought the man looked very sad. And close up he had a kind face.

Emma suddenly knew who he reminded her of. He looked just like Marjorie Wallace.

Sheltie began to give Mudlark a bath. He was licking the little donkey all over. And the more he cleaned the white donkey, the more the real black donkey showed through.

'A clever trick, covering the donkey in flour,' said PC Green. 'But you didn't fool Sheltie.'

Sheltie gave a loud snort when he heard his name.

'I'm going to arrest you for stealing this animal,' said the policeman. 'Have you anything to say for yourself?'

The old man looked ashamed and lowered his head.

'I'm very sorry,' he said. 'But I didn't really steal him. I was just taking him back.'

'Taking him back? What do you
mean?' asked Dad.

The old man said he was Todd
Wallace, Marjorie's brother.

So that's why he looks so much
like Marjorie, thought Emma.

Todd explained how, years ago, he

used to sell and deliver fresh fish to the villagers in Little Applewood.

'Mudlark and Sophie are brother and sister too,' he said. 'I used Mudlark to pull that very same fish cart through the streets.

'When I went off on my travels I left Mudlark behind with Marji. He was too frisky for a caravan and I couldn't look after two donkeys. And Marji did say that I could have Mudlark back whenever I wanted. She always knew I would come back for him one day.'

'But that was a long time ago,' said PC Green. 'And why didn't you tell Marjorie you were coming back for him and just *ask* instead of taking the donkey like that?'

Todd said that Marjorie was bossy and always trying to make him give up his life on the road.

'She wants me to settle down and live in a proper house,' he said. 'I had come to ask, but when I found out that Marji was away, I thought it would be much easier just to take Mudlark and explain later.' He looked at Emma and then at Dad.

'I know that it was wrong to take Mudlark from your paddock,' said Todd. 'But I only wanted Sophie to have some company in her old age. And a little help to pull the caravan.' He looked really sad.

'Well, what you say may be true, but you'll have to stay at the police station until Marjorie gets back and we clear up this mess,' said the policeman.

'One thing still bothers me though,' said Emma. 'If you weren't stealing Mudlark, why did you try to disguise him by covering him in flour?'

Todd lowered his head.

'I knew everyone would be looking for Mudlark. And I thought that if I disguised him then I could get away quietly without any fuss. I'm very sorry for all the trouble I've caused. I really am.'

PC Green drove Todd away in the back of the police car.

Chapter Thirteen

Dad said he would look after the caravan, Sophie and Tigger the cat. He climbed up into the driver's seat and took the reins. Slowly he turned Mudlark and Sophie around. Then he drove the caravan back up the slope to the top of the rise.

Emma followed behind in the fish cart, with Sheltie pulling it. Sheltie liked the little cart, and Emma thought it was fantastic, steering with the long reins.

They met Mrs Marsh on the crest of the hill. She seemed quite surprised to see Dad driving the caravan, with Emma and Sheltie following behind in the painted fish cart. She gave them a friendly wave and a big smile as they passed.

When they crossed Mr Brown's meadow and drove up the lane, little Joshua could hardly believe his eyes. He was waiting with Mum at the front gate, staring wide-eyed with amazement.

Once safely in the paddock, Dad freed Mudlark and Sophie from the caravan shafts.

Emma unharnessed Sheltie from

the fish cart, then went inside to fetch
a bucket of warm water from the
kitchen.

She got busy with soap and a soft
brush, and soon Mudlark was back to
his normal colour, as black as coal.

Sheltie galloped around the paddock,

chasing Sophie and Mudlark in a game of tag. Mum went inside for some carrots and apples.

'What's going to happen to Mr Wallace?' asked Emma. 'Will he go to prison? And who will look after Sophie?'

'I shouldn't think he will go to prison, seeing that he's Marjorie's brother, Emma. He seemed a nice old man really. And if what he said about Mudlark is true, then I suppose he didn't really steal the donkey anyway. But it was a silly thing to do. We'll have to wait until Marjorie gets back and see what she has to say. In the mean time, there's plenty of room in the paddock. That is, if Sheltie doesn't mind!'

Sheltie shook his mane and let out a long blow. He didn't mind at all.

A few days later, Marjorie came back from her holiday. Emma's dad picked her up from the train station and drove her home in the car.

When he sat Marjorie down and told her all the news, she could hardly believe her ears.

'Who would have thought that old Todd would turn up like that!' she said. 'I often think of him and wonder what he's up to, travelling around in that funny caravan all the time. He never did like living in one place in a proper house, like the rest of us. And he carries all his precious papers and things around in a silly old sack so he doesn't lose them.'

Marjorie was very worried about her brother being held at the police station. She asked Dad if he would drive her there straight away. She wanted to clear up this mess as quickly as possible.

Chapter Fourteen

That afternoon, Marjorie telephoned the cottage and asked if Emma and Sheltie would ride over after school. She said that she had some good news.

When Emma and Sheltie arrived, Marjorie was sitting out in the garden with her nine cats. She was very pleased to see Emma.

'You are such a clever girl, Emma,'

she said. 'And Sheltie is such a clever pony.'

Marjorie had been told all about Emma and Sheltie's adventure and how they had tracked down and found Mudlark.

'It was Sheltie really,' said Emma. 'He found all the clues – the cap and the piece of sock – and he led me to the caravan and Mudlark.'

'Oh yes, I mustn't forget,' said Marjorie, 'I've got a special present for Sheltie.' She went inside and came back with a beautiful leather saddle. It shone like a chestnut.

'This saddle used to belong to Mudlark. But nobody rides him any more. Todd gave me the saddle along with Mudlark and the little painted

fish cart over ten years ago when he
left. I think it will be just right for
Sheltie. It was Todd's idea.'

'Oh, thank you. It's lovely,' said
Emma. 'I'll keep it for Sunday best. It
can be Sheltie's Sunday saddle.'

Sheltie sniffed at the leather and

blew a loud raspberry of approval. He liked the Sunday saddle very much. Emma and Marjorie laughed. Sheltie could be so funny at times.

'What will happen to your brother?' asked Emma. 'And Sophie?'

Marjorie gave a big sigh.

'I'm afraid Todd is getting far too old to go off on his travels any more. I've sorted everything out with the police. And I've told Todd that Mudlark's and Sophie's caravan-pulling days are over, and that he's got to settle down.'

'Will he come and live here in Little Applewood?' asked Emma.

Sheltie pricked up his ears.

'I hope so,' said Marjorie. 'Or one of the nearby villages.'

'And will he take Mudlark?'

'That's the good news, Emma. Todd said I can have Mudlark for keeps. And Sophie too. I told Todd he will be able to come and visit them whenever he wants. But I hope he decides to come and live here with me. And I hope you and Sheltie will come and visit too, Emma.'

Sheltie pushed his muzzle into Marjorie's hand and blew hot air up her sleeve.

'That would be lovely,' laughed Emma.

'And we've found the missing kitten too,' said Marjorie. 'He'd gone and got himself locked inside the tool shed.'

Everything had turned out fine after all.

Mudlark and Sophie were in their
little field behind Marjorie's cottage.
Sheltie trotted over on his own and
rubbed noses with the two
donkeys.

'You're very lucky to have such a
clever pony, Emma,' said Marjorie.

'I know,' said Emma. 'Sheltie's the
best pony in the world.'

Choosing a brilliant book
can be a tricky business...
but not any more

www.puffin.co.uk

The best selection of books at your fingertips

So get clicking!

Searching the site is easy – you'll find
what you're looking for at the click of a mouse,
from great authors to brilliant books and more!

Everyone's got different taste . . .

I like stories that make me laugh

Animal stories are definitely my favourite

I'd say fantasy is the best

I like a bit of romance

It's got to be adventure for me

I really love poetry

I like a good mystery

Whatever you're into, we've got it covered . . .

www.puffin.co.uk

hotnews@puffin

Hot off the press!
You'll find all the latest exclusive Puffin news here

Where's it happening?
Check out our author tours and events programme

Best-sellers
What's hot and what's not? Find out in our charts

E-mail updates
Sign up to receive all the latest news
straight to your e-mail box

Links to the coolest sites
Get connected to all the best author web sites

Book of the Month
Check out our recommended reads

www.puffin.co.uk

www.puffin.co.uk.www.puffin.co.uk.www.puffin.co.uk
ookinfo.competitions.news.games.sneakpreviews
www.puffin.co.uk.www.puffin.co.uk.www.puffin.co.uk
dventure.bestsellers.fun.coollinks.freestuff
www.puffin.co.uk.www.puffin.co.uk.www.puffin.co.uk
xplore.yourshout.awards.toptips.authorinfo
www.puffin.co.uk.www.puffin.co.uk.www.puffin.co.uk
reatbooks.greatbooks.greatbooks.greatbooks
www.puffin.co.uk.www.puffin.co.uk.www.puffin.co.uk
eviews.poems.jokes.authorevents.audioclips
www.puffin.co.uk.www.puffin.co.uk.www.puffin.co.uk
nterviews.e-mailupdates.bookinfo.competitions.news

www.puffin.co.uk

ames.sneakpreviews.adventure.bestsellers.fun
www.puffin.co.uk.www.puffin.co.uk.www.puffin.co.uk
ookinfo.competitions.news.games.sneakpreviews
www.puffin.co.uk.www.puffin.co.uk.www.puffin.co.uk
dventure.bestsellers.fun.coollinks.freestuff
www.puffin.co.uk.www.puffin.co.uk.www.puffin.co.uk
xplore.yourshout.awards.toptips.authorinfo
www.puffin.co.uk.www.puffin.co.uk.www.puffin.co.uk
reatbooks.greatbooks.greatbooks.greatbooks
www.puffin.co.uk.www.puffin.co.uk.www.puffin.co.uk
eviews.poems.jokes.authorevents.audioclips
www.puffin.co.uk.www.puffin.co.uk.www.puffin.co.uk

Read more in Puffin

For complete information about books available from Puffin – and Penguin – and how to
order them, contact us at the appropriate address below. Please note that for copyright
reasons the selection of books varies from country to country.

www.puffin.co.uk

In the United Kingdom: Please write to Dept EP, Penguin Books Ltd,
Bath Road, Harmondsworth, West Drayton, Middlesex UB7 ODA

In the United States: Please write to Penguin Putnam Inc., P.O. Box 12289,
Dept B, Newark, New Jersey 07101–5289 or call 1–800–788–6262

In Canada: Please write to Penguin Books Canada Ltd,
10 Alcorn Avenue, Suite 300, Toronto, Ontario M4V 3B2

In Australia: Please write to Penguin Books Australia Ltd,
P.O. Box 257, Ringwood, Victoria 3134

In New Zealand: Please write to Penguin Books (NZ) Ltd,
Private Bag 102902, North Shore Mail Centre, Auckland 10

In India: Please write to Penguin Books India Pvt Ltd,
11 Panscheel Shopping Centre, Panscheel Park, New Delhi 110 017

In the Netherlands: Please write to Penguin Books Netherlands bv,
Postbus 3507, NL–1001 AH Amsterdam

In Germany: Please write to Penguin Books Deutschland GmbH,
Metzlerstrasse 26, 60594 Frankfurt am Main

In Spain: Please write to Penguin Books S. A., Bravo Murillo 19,
1° B, 28015 Madrid

In Italy: Please write to Penguin Italia s.r.l.,
Via Felice Casati 20, I–20124 Milano

In France: Please write to Penguin France S. A.,
17 rue Lejeune, F–31000 Toulouse

In Japan: Please write to Penguin Books Japan, Ishikiribashi Building,
2–5–4, Suido, Bunkyo-ku, Tokyo 112

In South Africa: Please write to Longman Penguin Southern Africa (Pty) Ltd,
Private Bag X08, Bertsham 2013